First published in Great Britain in 1992 by The Bodley Head Children's Books

This edition published in Great Britain in 2007 and in the USA in 2008 by
Frances Lincoln Children's Books, 4 Torriano Mews,
Torriano Avenue, London NW5 2RZ
www.franceslincoln.com

A catalogue record for this book is available from the Bristish Library.

ISBN 978-1-84507-721-1

Printed in Jurong Town, Singapore by Star Standard Industries in August 2011
9 8 7 6 5 4

DOING THE GARDEN

Sarah Garland

F
FRANCES LINCOLN
CHILDREN'S BOOKS

Spring has come.

We'll push the old pram

to the garden shop.

There are plants and

seeds and bushes

It is rather big.

And it is a long way home.

We must plant the flowers

and sow the seeds

and plant some sticks

and bury some bones...

and dig them up again.

Let's dig a deep hole,

deeper and deeper.

Gently, gently, in it goes.

What a beautiful tree!